Isabella's Above-Ground Pool

Also by Alice Mead

Junebug
Adem's Cross
Junebug and the Reverend
Soldier Mom
Girl of Kosovo
Junebug in Trouble
Year of No Rain
Madame Squidley and Beanie
Swimming to America

Isabella's Above-Ground Pool

Alice Mead

Pictures by **Maryann Cocca-Leffler**

Farrar, Straus and Giroux
New York

www.fsgkidsbooks.com

Library of Congress Cataloging-in-Publication Data
Mead, Alice.
    Isabella's above-ground pool / Alice Mead ; pictures by Maryann
Cocca-Leffler.— 1st ed.
        p.   cm.
    Summary: Nine-year-old Isabella's motto is "I won't share 'cuz it's
not fair," until a tornado destroys a neighbor's house and she realizes
that the money she has earned to buy a swimming pool might be
put to a better use.
    ISBN-13: 978-0-374-33617-2
    ISBN-10: 0-374-33617-2
    1. Sharing—Fiction.   2. Swimming pools—Fiction.
3. Tornadoes—Fiction.   4. Texas—Fiction.   I. Cocca-Leffler,
Maryann, date, ill.   II. Title.

PZ7.M47887 Is 2006
[Fic]—dc22

                                                    2004051473

*For Beverly Reingold
and Elaine Chubb*

Isabella's Above-Ground Pool

1

Isabella **Speedwalker-Juarez** stood in the middle of the mobile home's tiny bedroom, dropped her duffel bag and backpack, and slowly turned all the way around just to be sure. "Nope. This won't work. Hey, Mom?" she called.

"What, Belly?" asked her little brother, Dozer.

"This is awful. Where can I put my armadillo collection? Or my soccer ball? My comic books? My inflatable Tyrannosaurus rex? Oh, Mom? Yoo-hoo! This room is way too small for two of us! I told you that before we moved here, and I'm telling you again!"

"Hush, Izzy, sweetie. I think it'll be all right," said her mother as she hurried in. "Granny Speedwalker bought you and Dozer these bunk beds, and I'm sure we can find a way to fit in your things."

"Mom! No! I need my own room! I can't live squashed into a tiny room with a toddler!"

"Where there's a will, there's a way. You can share a room easily enough."

"No I can't! I hate sharing. Sharing is what grownups make kids do when they're stuck with a bad deal. A nine-year-old girl can't share a room

3

with a two-year-old!" Isabella had just turned nine and Dozer was almost three, but what difference did that make?

Isabella burst into tears. Because she was crying, Dozer sat down on the floor and cried, too.

"Oh, lordy. Come here," their mother said, scooping up the little boy. "Isabella, sit by me on the lower bunk. See, now? Isn't this cozy?"

"No." Isabella sniffled. "It isn't. Why can't I have my own room? Dozer will get into everything. Maybe I can live next door, in Zach's toolshed or something." Isabella hoped her pathetic sniffles would make her mother relent.

"Don't be silly. You're not moving in with a neighbor. I've explained this to you a hundred times. Granny has her hair-cutting salon in the large bedroom, so Granny and I will share the medium-sized bedroom, and you and Dozer will just have to share this one. That's all there is to it."

Isabella stuck out her bottom lip. "I am *not* happy. This is Mr. Wigglesworth's fault for cutting your hours at the factory. Where's the phone? I'm calling him right now and giving him a piece of my mind."

"Please try to calm down, Izzy. He really can't do anything about it. Everyone's hours were reduced,

4

not just mine. The Longnose Gum factory is in big trouble. I'm lucky to have a job at all."

"Humph." Isabella sulked, wondering what she could do.

Meanwhile, Dozer had slid off the bed and was lugging Isabella's inflatable Tyrannosaurus around by the neck, chanting, "Big, bad teef. Big, bad teef."

Isabella and her mom laughed. Then Dozer stumbled and fell. The dinosaur popped. Slowly the air hissed out.

"Dozer!" shouted Isabella. "You see, Mom? You see what he did?"

"Well, I'm sorry. But he didn't do it on purpose, for heaven's sake!" her mother said.

Granny Speedwalker popped her head into the room. Tight gray curls sprang from her head, and she wore orange rubber gloves to keep the permanent chemicals off her fingers.

"Would y'all keep the noise down? Deborah's mother is here, and she wants some kind of fancy Hollywood-style makeover. This trailer sounds like a bad day in the barnyard. Now, hush!"

"Sorry, Mother," Isabella's mom said, and quietly closed the door. Then she turned to Isabella. "You are too strong-willed for your own good, Izzy. I couldn't afford to keep us in our old house. We have

to stay here for now. I know the room is tiny. I know Granny isn't used to having us. And I know you didn't want to change schools. But that's just how things are."

Uh-oh. School! She had forgotten about school. She could stand school better when she played sports.

"I spent three years working my way up from the Pee Wee League in East Longnose, but there's no soccer team here," Isabella said with a big sigh. "I'll go nuts."

"Maybe there's tennis. Or some gymnastics program that you could join."

"No way. Hey! What about that pool we have on layaway? Let's set that up ASAP. Never mind this, Mom. Let's just go get that pool, okay?" Isabella jumped to her feet.

Her mother didn't answer immediately. Instead she began neatly laying Dozer's overalls in his drawer. "Er, I don't think so. Not today. Let's unpack the rest of your things."

"We can go later, right?"

Isabella's mom simply handed her a box of stuffed animals to put away.

But just as Isabella had feared, when she unloaded her collection of stuffed armadillos onto the floor of the closet, Dozer happily flopped down on top of them. Then, when she lined up her books on the tiny bookshelf in the room, Dozer busily pulled them down onto the floor. And he noisily tromped back and forth with the now-flattened dinosaur, singing the big-bad-teeth song.

"Dozer, listen! The closet is mine, so stay out of there. And I'm taking the bottom bunk, so you better not—"

"Izzy, no. I need you to take the top bunk. Dozer can't possibly sleep up there. What if he rolled off?"

Isabella opened her eyes wide and stared at her mom. The top bunk? She'd be staring at the ceiling. She'd sit up too fast and bonk her head. But what was the use of arguing? She knew Dozer wouldn't be safe up there. Quickly she yanked her clothes out of the suitcases. Some she hung in the closet, and the rest she stuffed into the two top dresser drawers, which were the only ones she could have. The rest were for Dozer, of course.

Then she ran outside to visit the neighbors.

2

Because they had moved from East Longnose, Isabella knew the funny thing about Center Long-nose, a tiny town in central Texas, was that nearly everyone in town had an unusual name. Like Granny Speedwalker. The Speedwalkers were famous for their fast walk. And then there was the Longnose family, which had first settled here in 1848. There were the Pettifoggers, the Wigglesworths, the Bad-deals, and the Nibblebitzes, among others. Her new teacher for third grade was going to be Mrs. Evalina Longnose Wigglesworth, who was sister-in-law to Isabella's mother's boss, Ernest Wigglesworth.

Deborah Nibblebitz-Fifer lived across the street. Deborah was almost nine, and pretty nice, and prob-ably Isabella's only friend at the moment. She'd of-fered to help Isabella get used to her new school.

Next door, over the split-rail fence, lived the town handyman, Zachary Joe O'Toole, who special-ized in repairing riding mowers. He had the absolute greatest backyard, filled with an old car chassis with a steering wheel, rusty motors, and tires piled high. The yard had a carousel horse with only three legs and a fourth one lying in the tall grass, a small cement mixer full of hardened lumps of old cement, and a boat on a trailer. The boat had a big hole in the side that was maybe from a crash, probably a shipwreck involving scuba divers.

A sign on his garage said ZACH O'TOOLE'S FIX-IT SHOP. OUR MOTTO: I CAN IF YOU CAN'T.

Well, now, thought Isabella, staring at the sign. A motto. That was a good idea. It told everyone exactly where you stood. Maybe she would make herself a motto, too. She'd tell the world precisely how she felt about sharing.

But what about that fix-it part? How could Zach fix things other people couldn't? Then she had a brilliant idea: could he make an extra bedroom, one just for her?

Isabella ran across the yard and climbed the fence. "Hey, howdy!" she called out, peering into the coolness of the rickety fix-it shop. She'd met Zach many times before while visiting her granny.

"Hellooo out there," called a voice. A tall, gangly man wearing a green John Deere cap came to the door. "Howdy, Isabella. Good to see you. What can I do you for?"

"We just moved in next door. But right off the bat, I have a big problem. I need some fix-it help.

Could you make my bedroom bigger or build me a brand-new one?" Isabella asked.

"Where's your room?" Zach pushed his cap back off his forehead and looked over at the trailer.

"Right there. Last window." She pointed at Granny Speedwalker's trailer. "Dozer and I have to share a room. One tiny room! He's ruining my stuff! He exploded my dinosaur and leaped on my armadillos. It's just not going to work."

"The back corner bedroom?"

"Yep. Two of us. We absolutely do not fit."

"No. I wouldn't think you would. I'm sorry, Isabella, but I can't make that room bigger."

"Your motto says you fix stuff when other people can't."

"Not in this case. I'd have to knock out Granny's outside wall on that trailer, build a cement slab, run out new wiring, change the roofline. Nope. Can't do it. Can't make you any smaller either."

"Shoot."

"There's probably other ways to solve that dilemma."

"Like what?"

"We'll think of an alternative. Something we *can* do."

Think about something else? Why did grownups

always talk that way? Isabella narrowed her eyes. "Can I live here in your fix-it shop? I wouldn't be in the way, I promise."

Zach looked thoughtful. "Well, that's one alternative. But it kind of makes me the one to fix your problem, don't you think? I bet there are much better Isabella-style solutions to be found."

"No, there aren't."

"First off, whoever said bedrooms end at outside walls?" Zach asked.

Isabella plunked down on the ground and pulled up a stalk of timothy, lightly running it up and down her leg, while Zach went back to fixing a large green riding mower. He tipped it up on its side. The big blade looked like a ceiling fan coated with matted grass.

What on earth did Zach mean? Set up a tent? She could live in that, but not when it rained. Or maybe he meant build a tree house. But that was so much hard work. Lugging old boards up a tree. Getting splinters. Hammering your thumb. Ouch.

No, Isabella decided, it was too hard to come up with something entirely new. It was so much easier to pester people until they caved in and did what you wanted. That was the route to go.

She was going to have a motto, the way Zach did.

Hers would be "I won't share 'cuz it's not fair!" If she kept saying that, maybe her mom would move Dozer into her own much bigger bedroom.

"I gotta go now. See ya later, Zach," she said, scrambling to her feet. "It's motto time!"

3

Minutes later, Isabella sat at Granny's kitchen table, drawing the outlines of the letters for her motto. She wrote I WON'T SHARE 'CUZ IT'S NOT FAIR in big, messy, wobbly letters, each one a different color.

Dozer leaned against her leg, watching. "Can I draw, too, Belly?" he asked.

"Sure. Mom gave you some chunky crayons. You can go draw with those. Now scoot."

After she had taped the signs to the refrigerator, the back door, her bedroom door, the bathroom door, and the medicine cabinet, she felt restless and twitchy. She yelled for her mother. "Yoo-hoo, Mom! Take a look at my motto. What do you think?"

Her mother came in with a basket full of laundry and stood in front of the refrigerator, reading. "What is this, Izzy?"

"I'm protesting. You guys aren't listening to me, so I decided to have a motto like Zach."

"Isn't his motto about helping people fix things?"

"Well, yeah."

"And yours is about helping yourself to more than your share?"

"No it's not!" Izzy argued hotly. "You just don't get it."

"Hold on here. What's this? There's another one in the hallway?"

"Yep. They're all over the house," Izzy said proudly.

"I think you should take them down," her mother said.

"Nope."

"As soon as you are able would be nice."

"No way."

Izzy went to her room and closed the door. She sat on the armadillos inside her closet. Once Isabella got worked up about something, it took her a long, long time to settle down again. Sometimes listening to music helped. Sometimes rocking in a rocking chair helped. But that was what she did at her old house. She had no idea what to do here.

The closet was too hot. So she climbed onto her top bunk and stared at a spidery stain on the ceiling. She was lying stock still, like a mummy in a coffin. Even that wasn't calming her one bit.

Maybe she needed to run around and exercise her speedy Speedwalker legs. She could run over to Deborah's. But no, now she remembered that Deborah wasn't home. Granny had told her that Deborah was over at her dad's for the day. Isabella had a dad, too, but she couldn't visit him. He'd left for California soon after Dozer had been born.

The problem right now was fixing her bedroom. She couldn't remove Dozer, and Zach couldn't expand the room. There were other ways, he had said.

Isabella's thoughts returned to the pool. They could put the pool right outside her bedroom window. She could make a plastic chute running from her window right down into it. Any time she felt hot or tired or needed to get away, she could climb out the bedroom window and slide *kersploosh!* into the cool water. Then she would have the best bedroom in the whole world!

"Mom?" She sat up and banged her head on the ceiling. "Ouch. Mom?"

Her mother was sitting on the back steps of the deck, reading *Goodnight Moon* to Dozer in the hope that he would soon take one of his famous power naps. Once he fell asleep, Dozer could sleep through anything.

"Mom!" Isabella yelped, rushing out the door. "We have to go to Ray's. We have to buy the pool. Then I can make this spectacular combination bedroom/pool/indoor/outdoor—"

"Shhh! Granny has a customer."

"Oh. Sorry. But, about the pool? Can we get it today?"

Her mother looked uncomfortable. "We already talked about that. Besides, it's April first, Isabella. We don't need that pool right now, do we?"

"You said we'd still finish paying for it no matter what. You said that, Mom. That was the deal about moving here. You said when Granny was busy, we could play in the pool. Remember that?"

Her mother sighed. "I did say that. But our old house isn't sold yet, Izzy. We just don't have four hundred dollars to spare."

Disappointed, Isabella sank down on the wooden steps. First half of a tiny bedroom and now no pool? "When will you have the money?" she asked in a small voice.

"I don't know. I'm afraid to promise you anything right now, in case things don't turn out quite the way we hope."

"I hate that Mr. Wigglesworth," Isabella said. "I'm mad at him."

"Yeah," said her mom. "I'm pretty mad, too."

"You are?" Isabella said in surprise.

Her mom nodded.

"Let's close our eyes and be really, really mad," suggested Isabella.

So she and her mom sat on the steps and closed their eyes. When they opened them again, they saw that Dozer had finally fallen asleep in his mom's lap.

"Awww. Look at him. Isn't he cute?" her mom asked.

Dozer was a cute kid. Even cuter when he was sleeping, because his cheeks looked extra round and rosy and his dark hair got a little bit curlier. Isabella's mother stood up carefully, tiptoed into the bedroom, and gently laid Dozer on the bottom bunk, quietly closing the door.

"And now the bedroom is off limits, right, while he naps?" Isabella said.

"Yes."

"You do see that this is unfair?"

"Yes. But I also see, especially from your motto, that you are thinking about yourself a lot and hardly thinking at all about how you can give to others."

"Give? Give? I don't think so."

"My point exactly," Isabella's mom said.

Deborah's mother, Mrs. Nibblebitz-Fifer, came out to the back door. "Well, ladies? What do you think of my new look? Stylish, isn't it?"

"Very nice," said Isabella's mom.

"It's okay. Can Deborah play later?" Isabella asked.

"I'm afraid not. She usually gets home from her

dad's around eight. And then it's a bath and to bed at nine."

"Oh. Bed at nine. Yikes. Well, tell her I said howdy."

"I will. Bye, now."

When Mrs. Nibblebitz-Fifer had left, Isabella said, "I'm having a very bad day, Mom."

Her mom hugged her. "I'm sorry. But you know what else is bad? I'm sharing a bed, a double bed, with my own mother! And she snores!"

Isabella smiled and wrinkled her nose. "Poor you."

"I'll say. If you want to get away from Dozer, I'd be willing to trade with you. You can sleep with Granny. That top bunk looks fine to me."

"No way! I'll be okay. Really, Mom."

Her mother laughed.

4

After lunch, Isabella and her mother heard the creak of the mailbox at the front door. Granny appeared at the back door with a letter addressed to Joann Speedwalker-Juarez.

Isabella seized it. "Look, Mom. Our first letter at Granny's house. That's cool."

It was from Discount Ray's Bargain Warehouse in downtown Longnose.

March 30, 2000

Dear Joann Speedwalker-Juarez,

This is to notify you that you have had our last full-sized above-ground pool on layaway for over ONE YEAR. Layaway is not intended to be a PERMANENT STATE OF AFFAIRS. If we do not receive $400 by the end of April 2000, your money will be returned and you can kiss that pool goodbye.

Regards,
Raymond Baddeal
Owner and Manager

"We'll never get the money in time," wailed Isabella. "Oh, Mom."

"Those Baddeals are a bunch of low-down skunks," Granny said. "I'd shave every one of 'em bald if I had the chance."

"We're getting that pool," Isabella's mother said. "We're not sitting here squealing like stuck pigs. Come on, Izzy, get the coffee can. I'll get dressed. Then we're heading downtown."

Isabella found the can where they kept the above-ground pool fund in the kitchen. She peered inside. It held $6.37, which was two weeks of her allowance plus 37 cents that Dozer had found under Granny's armchair.

"This isn't going to help much, Mom," Isabella said fretfully.

"No. But I'll write him a check for two hundred. That ought to hold him. And you pay him the $6.37. Every penny helps! Now come on. Granny can watch Dozer if he wakes up before we get back."

Isabella's mother stepped out, looking both mad and snazzy in see-through plastic high-heel sandals and pink polka-dot capri pants. Isabella hot-footed it along behind.

Isabella couldn't wait to get that pool into the backyard. Once she did, she'd be lounging in it all by herself, as cool as a cucumber. All the other kids would be jealous and would beg for a chance to come in. But she wouldn't let them. Nosiree! The pool would be just hers, her watery, private, beyond-the-walls bedroom.

Yes. Floating in her pool, the water holding her like a liquid blanket, she would feel safe and secure. It wouldn't matter about the gum factory, or losing her bedroom, or not being on a soccer team. The pool would be a whole new place just for her.

But she was daydreaming too much. Her mother was getting way ahead of her. Isabella shifted her skinny legs into high gear and barreled after her mother, still no match for the rapid click-clack of her plastic sandals.

As they neared the discount store, they passed two boys on bikes, Nicky Ramsbottom and Marco Popovich. Isabella had met them when she'd visited Center Longnose Elementary.

"Hey, Isabella, wait up!" Nicky hollered.

"Can't!" Isabella panted.

"Where are you going? Slow down!"

The boys were now pedaling furiously after them.

"To Discount Ray's, to put some more money down on our swimming pool."

"Wow! You're getting a pool? Can we swim in it?" Nicky asked as they pulled alongside.

"Nope. No way," Isabella gasped breathlessly.

"What? Why not?"

" 'Cause. Nobody can but me. I don't share. I don't believe in it. In fact, my motto is 'I don't share 'cuz it's not fair.' So there. Now quit following me. My mom and I have some very important business to take care of."

Luckily, Isabella's mother didn't hear her being so unfriendly. Except for Discount Ray, people in both East and Center Longnose prided themselves on their friendliness. Isabella's rudeness stuck out like a sore thumb.

Isabella and her mother entered the store and headed for Ray's office in the back. Isabella wanted to barge right in. But mean old Ray was chatting on the phone and held up one finger to show them they should wait. Isabella stared at him through the large office window. Ray Baddeal had slicked-back hair and a pencil-thin mustache. He wore suspenders over his starched white shirt.

Izzy stared at him as hard as she could, making her face fierce and mean, trying to send him an ESP message that would make him turn nice for a few minutes and say, Sure, Isabella. I'm sorry I wrote you that letter. I'll tear it up right now. Take that pool today. Pay me off whenever you get the chance. But maybe ESP didn't work through glass, because Ray Baddeal just blathered on and on.

As she waited, Isabella noticed a stack of plastic wading pools for toddlers piled on the shop floor. "Look, Mom. Little wading pools. For toddlers."

"How cute. Hey, I know!" said Isabella's mom. "Dozer's birthday is coming next Saturday. We should get him one, don't you think? They're only a few dollars. Oh, Ray's off the phone. Now, Izzy, stay out of my way. You wait for me up at the register while I give Raymond Baddeal a piece of my mind."

Isabella dragged herself to the front of the store and peered into the gumball machine. She needed a quarter for some gum, but she couldn't use her pool money. She frowned and smacked the side of the machine to see if one would roll out by accident. Isabella wasn't pleased about getting Dozer a pool for his third birthday, not when she'd been hoping and waiting for one whole year for a great big one. How unfair would that be?

Her mother came speeding up to the register carrying the wading pool. She opened her Elvis Presley plastic purse and plunked down a ten-dollar bill and a two-hundred-dollar check along with Isabella's money. "The two hundred six thirty-seven is for our pool on layaway," she told the clerk. She took her receipt, then snatched up the wading pool, seized Isabella by the arm, and whirled her around. "Here.

Carry this. Come on, kiddo, let's move it," she muttered.

Isabella took the toddler pool. "But, Mom, what did Ray Baddeal say? Can we have more time?"

"He said he'd be nice and give us until May. Our deadline is now May first. He gave us one more day."

"May first?" wailed Isabella. "But how can we possibly—"

"You hush up about this, now, Izzy. We will discuss this pool business in the privacy of our own home," her mother said. "But, oooh, I'm fit to be tied."

They pushed through the door, back out into the glare and heat of a central Texas afternoon. Isabella stopped in the middle of the sidewalk. "Wow. It's hot."

There were Nicky and Marco, sitting on their bikes, waiting. When they saw Isabella carrying the toddler pool, the boys burst out laughing.

"Ha, ha, ha! Wait a minute!" Marco pointed at the plastic pool. "That's it? That's your swimming pool, Isabella?"

"Of course it's not!" Isabella said. "Mine's an above-ground pool on layaway. This is for Dozer, my little brother. So quit laughing, you guys!"

"Let's see you swim in that little thing!" Nicky said.

"Yeah, it's six inches deep," said Marco. "Hope you don't drown! Come on, Nicky. Let's go. See you at school on Monday!"

"Yeah. See you." Glumly, Isabella looked after them as they rode away.

"Are those boys in your class, Isabella?" her mother asked.

"Unfortunately."

"Now, now," said her mother. "I'm sure they're very nice boys once you get to know them. You could try to be a little bit friendlier."

Act friendly to Nicky and Marco? Isabella wondered if her mom came from another planet.

The walk home was roasting hot. Isabella's bangs stuck to her sweaty forehead, and she stomped along in a foul mood. She carried the pool upside down, perched on top of her head like a gigantic turquoise hat.

"Gosh!" her mother said as they reached their driveway. "It's hot enough to fry an egg on the sidewalk and it's only April first. It's going to be one long summer for sure."

That made Isabella even more determined to get the pool. She had to earn some money if old man Baddeal wasn't going to cooperate. She needed two hundred smackeroos, and fast.

Maybe she could sell lemonade. But everyone did

that. At ten cents a cup, it would take all spring and summer to raise the money.

What about a car wash? High school kids did it all the time to raise money for football and cheerleading. She could easily clean the bumpers, lights, the grilles. But could she wash the car roofs all by herself? She'd find a way.

Yes. A car wash would do it. Two dollars a car. She could start tomorrow. Lots of people probably wanted their cars washed on a Sunday, so they could get that nasty Texas dust off for church.

5

By Sunday, the spell of hot weather had passed. It was cool and rainy, not a car-washing day. So after Granny served them a pancake breakfast, Isabella went over to Zach's to tell him all about Ray Baddeal and Nicky and Marco.

Zach was in his fix-it shop, even though it was Sunday. Spring was his busiest season.

"Still working on that banged-up riding mower, Zach?" Isabella asked.

"Yep. I can't set this blade in there right. It keeps scraping on the casing. The owner rode over a rock with the mower and bent the goldurned casing all out of whack."

"Listen, Zach. About my bedroom? I had this great idea," Isabella said. "Instead of trying to make it bigger, which you said we can't, I was thinking I could sort of add to it on the outside."

"Great thinking," Zach commented. "How are you going to do that?"

"When I get my above-ground pool, I can build a slide out my bedroom window from my top bunk into the pool, so the pool can be my special get-away place. But we still owe money, and if we don't pay off that two hundred dollars soon, Discount Ray won't let us have the pool."

"Hmm. Sounds like you're in a worse fix today than you were yesterday."

"No. Because guess what."

"No idea."

"I'm going to open a car wash and wash cars every weekend, unless it rains like today. I'll earn that pool money all by myself."

"Is that so?" Zach asked. "Isabella's Car Wash. Very commendable."

"Yeah. And guess what else."

"No idea."

"I have school tomorrow with these two awful teasy boys, Nicky Ramsbottom and Marco Popovich, but I won't care if they tease because Deborah's walking me. My teacher's Mrs. Wigglesworth."

"Okay, yeah. Nicky and Marco. Well, Deborah's a real nice girl. Smart, too. And Mrs. Wigglesworth? I think you'll like her. She tries hard to be fair to everybody. Yep. She's a great lady. I had her in the third grade myself."

"You did? How long ago was that?"

"Oh, back when dinosaurs roamed the earth."

"Yoo-hoo! Izzy?" Isabella's mom, holding an umbrella above her head, was leaning across Granny's fence. "Let Zach have time to work, now."

"Come on over, Mom!" Isabella hollered. "He's not busy."

"Not so you'd notice, I guess." Zach laughed.

Isabella's mom tossed the umbrella over and climbed the fence. "Howdy, Zach," she said.

"Hey, Joann. Isabella was telling me about your layaway problem down at Ray's."

"What a stingy man. We've been making those pool payments—most of them, anyway—since last year. Izzy will be so disappointed if we can't get the pool after waiting so long."

"I'm going to earn the rest of that money, Mom. I'm going to have a car wash. Zach, you got any hoses lying around?"

"Three of 'em. Hanging on the wall on those brackets." He pointed with a big screwdriver.

"Oh, yeah. I see." Isabella lifted a hose off the wall. It was heavier than it looked. She clutched it to her chest and staggered out into the steady drizzle, uncoiling it. She wanted to see if it would reach the street.

"Are you sure it's okay if she uses your hoses?" her mother asked Zach. "Taking them out in the rain and everything?"

"Oh, shoot, sure. Hoses are made to get wet."

"All right, then. I have to get back to Dozer."

One at a time, Isabella laid out Zach's hoses end to end. The third one reached the street. Deborah must have been watching from her front window because she came out in a red rain slicker and yellow boots.

"Hey, Deborah. I'm making a car wash place here at Zach's driveway because I need to earn some money."

"What for?"

"An above-ground pool," Isabella said.

"Wow. I'll help you wash cars," Deborah said.

Zach strolled up behind Isabella. "Now, look at that. Already you have a helper."

Isabella didn't say anything. She liked Deborah, and Mrs. Wigglesworth was seating them near each other in class so Isabella could sit with someone she knew. But wouldn't Deborah expect to swim in the pool if she helped Isabella earn the money? Of course she would. She might even bring her friends. A whole crowd of people might turn up!

"You look perturbed, Isabella. What's up?" Zach asked.

"I *am* perturbed. 'Cause, well, see, I wasn't planning on sharing the pool with anybody," she mumbled in an embarrassed voice. "So maybe it would be best if Deborah didn't help with the car wash."

No one spoke. Deborah's eyes filled with tears. "Then I guess I'll go home."

Isabella nodded and watched Deborah walk down the driveway, step over the hoses, and return home. She felt so ashamed. But she desperately wanted one private place all to herself.

Keeping her face turned away from Zach, Isabella slowly gathered up the hoses, coiled them, and hung them back on the wall brackets of the workshop where she'd found them.

"Well, Isabella," Zach said finally, "I don't know quite what to say. Seems like you hurt Deborah's feelings pretty bad. Now, I don't understand that. Why would you do such a thing?"

His quiet tone upset Isabella more than if he'd just sent her directly home or yelled at her.

"I don't know. Yes, I do. 'Cause nobody cares about my feelings. They just do whatever they want and tell me to get used to it. That's why. I didn't want to move to Granny's. I didn't want my dad to leave. I didn't even want a baby brother. And I don't want to share a tiny room with Dozer!" By now she was practically shouting.

"Guess you're a pretty angry kid," Zach observed, getting back to work.

"Yeah." Isabella flopped down onto the seat of a small red riding mower. A few minutes passed.

"I'm worried about tomorrow," Zach said. "How did you say you're getting to school?"

"I'm walking with Deborah."

"I thought so. How do you think that's going to go after what just happened here?"

Isabella pressed her lips tightly together. She got off the red riding mower. She knew she should talk to Deborah. "I guess I'd better get going now."

"See ya," Zach called out. "Stop over anytime."

Instead of heading directly home, Isabella crossed the street and knocked on Deborah's door. Deborah opened it. "Oh! Hi, Isabella."

Isabella was relieved that Deborah hadn't said anything rude or mean to her. "Hi. I—umm—I came over to apologize. I really do want you to swim in my pool. And it's very nice of you to offer to walk me to school and stuff."

"Yeah. Sure. It's terrible being a new kid."

Isabella smiled. "At least I'm from East Longnose, so I'm used to the funny names around here. How's Mrs. Wigglesworth, anyway? Is she strict?"

"No!" Deborah laughed. "She hates name-calling, though. So whatever you do, don't call anyone a name. Even a tiny name, like 'idiot' or 'dum-dum.' Nothing."

"I'll try to remember. What about messiness?"

"She hates messiness."

"Uh-oh. I'm in trouble." Isabella sighed. "My handwriting is so messy."

"You want to come in?"

"I guess. My little brother's probably still taking his nap. We're sharing a room. That's why I'm in a kind of bad mood. If he's napping, I have no place to hang out. Hey! You want to help make advertisements for my car wash? We can say it'll be next weekend."

"Sure. I'll get my markers and some paper."

So they each made an ad with the location of the car wash, Zachary O'Toole's driveway. They posted them on the telephone poles at the end of their road. Isabella had fun, until it was time to go back to the crowded trailer. And she felt bad again about sharing the pool. What if Nicky and Marco joined in once they saw her and Deborah splashing around? Things could get out of hand. She just wanted some control over her life. Was that too much to ask?

"Deborah, it's fine for you to share the pool. But nobody else, okay? I want to keep it like a secret club just for us."

Deborah looked at her in a funny way. "Well, okay," she said. "If that's how you want it. See you to-morrow."

6

On Monday morning, when Isabella and Deborah arrived at school, Isabella found that Nicky and Marco had done a pretty good job of telling everyone how she had *said* she was getting an above-ground pool but had come out of Discount Ray's with a toddler pool instead. A lot of kids, boys mostly, were whispering and laughing at her. She raised her head high and paraded right past them. But a line of boys followed her, chanting, "Toddler pool. Toddler pool. Pee oh oh ell."

"Cut it out, you guys," Deborah said. "Get out of here."

The boys burst out laughing and ran away.

"I'm going to swing," Isabella said.

"Not me. I'm just going to sit under the tree and read," said Deborah.

Isabella waltzed confidently over to the swing. Because of her long legs, she had been famous for her high swinging at her old school. But Nicky was already on the swing, and tiny Center Longnose Elementary had only one. Isabella was determined to be on it.

"Hey, Nicky! I want to swing. It's my turn!" she commanded.

"Don't boss, okay? You'll have to wait."

So Nicky kept swinging up and back, up and back. Finally Isabella grabbed ahold of one of the cables, and the swing lurched to a stop.

"Hey!" Nicky hollered. "Let go!"

"Nope. My turn, I said!"

Nicky tried to pry her fingers loose. Quickly Isabella grabbed the other cable as well and jumped onto the back of the swing, standing up, with Nicky still on it. "There. Now we can both swing."

"We can, but isn't that sharing?" Nicky asked slyly.

"Well, yes. But it's sharing by you, not by me."

"Good grief. Oh, all right," Nicky grumbled, pushing the swing back with his toes.

"Higher," ordered Isabella. "I want to go higher."

Marco ran past them, headed for the door. He skidded to a halt in front of the swing. "Ohhh," he said. "Look at that. How cute. Nicky and Isabella sitting in a tree, K-I-S-S-I-N-G—"

"Marco! Cut it out!" Nicky said.

"You guys are going to be soooo late," said Marco. "The first bell just rang." And he dashed off.

Nicky leaped from the swing and ran, too.

"Wait up! Wait, you guys!" Isabella was yelling.

She glanced over at the tree, but Deborah had already gone inside.

Isabella's feet pounded past Nicky in a speedwalk, beating him to the door. By now the second morning bell was already ringing. Isabella and Nicky were indeed late. They rushed down the hall to their third-grade classroom.

"Come on! But don't run, Nicky, or we could get in trouble!" Isabella called over her shoulder.

"I'm—not—running!" Nicky gasped, trying his best to keep up.

They rounded the corner at top speed and pushed open the door to Room 13. Marco, Deborah, and the other children were all in their seats.

"Sorry, Mrs. Wigglesworth," Nicky and Isabella sang out. Quickly they took their seats.

Mrs. Wigglesworth had arranged the class so that everyone sat in a group of four desks pushed together. Isabella's group had Nicky, Marco, and Deborah. Only Jimmy Pettifogger was not part of a group. He sat in the back by himself because he had a habit of calling out. Each desk was neatly labeled, so Isabella had no trouble figuring out who was who.

The day's schedule was written on the board in very neat cursive. Isabella's heart sank. "Neatness is not your strength," her other teacher had told her often enough. No one seemed to like Isabella's smudgy, smeary, tipping-over letters and the rips on the math pages, which was what happened if she erased too much in one place.

Isabella was basically a slob. Her thoughts strayed to her bedroom. Already her armadillos had escaped from their closet hideout and were strewn everywhere. Crayons were scattered all over the floor, clothes flung about, and bed linens rumpled.

She heard Mrs. Wigglesworth say something about discussing a kickball tournament with the fourth grade. Next Mrs. Wigglesworth reviewed the early morning schedule. Spelling was first. Then cursive practice. Then reading.

"Exactly the same schedule as in my old school," Isabella said out loud.

"We raise our hands at Center Longnose, dear," said Mrs. Wigglesworth. She had white, frizzy hair and a long bumpy nose with reading glasses perched on the very end.

"Yeah, Isabella," Marco echoed. "Raise your hand. And, for your information, we take turns on the swing." Then he jumped up and did a little hula dance beside his desk, singing, "Isabelly, belly, belly, doesn't share the bread and jelly."

Jed Wafflefoote, a tall boy at the next group of desks, snorted with laughter. "Isabelly, belly, belly," he whispered. Isabella glared at him. "Doesn't share the bread and jelly."

"Voices. Voices." Mrs. Wigglesworth looked over. "Jed? Is there a problem?"

"No, ma'am," he said.

Marco sat down fast.

"I want it quiet," Mrs. Wigglesworth said. "We cannot talk about the third-and-fourth-grade kickball game until I have quiet."

Everyone immediately stopped whispering. Isabella looked around. This game was obviously a very big deal.

"Now, about kickball . . ."

The class broke out in an uproar of begging. "Pick me, Mrs. Wigglesworth. Can I be captain? Please!" called out Jimmy.

"And can I be pitcher? Please!" said Jed, his arm raised.

"Yeah!" shouted Marco. "Pick Jed for pitcher. We'll cream those fourth graders if Jed pitches."

Nicky, who was pretty good at art, held up a sign drawn in red crayon that read JED FOR PITCHER! and, below that, GET AHEAD WITH JED!

Other kids raised their hands, too, begging to be pitcher. Isabella had her hand up, but she wasn't pleading. Instead, she had put an expression of silent suffering on her face.

Now the boys were waving JED FOR PITCHER signs like Nicky's, and they began to chant, "Jed's the best, Jed's the best."

"All right!" exclaimed Mrs. Wigglesworth. "That's quite enough! Jimmy Pettifogger will be team captain, and let's see, we need a girl . . ." Her eyes roved the classroom. There was dead silence. "Isabella, our new girl, will be pitcher. That's only fair."

"Fair?" asked Nicky. "I don't think so."

The other boys all groaned loudly. Someone even booed.

"We're doomed," Marco moaned. He laid his head on his desk in obvious despair.

"Mrs. Wigglesworth, those kids are a year older than we are. We can't win unless we have a great pitcher," Jed said.

"Excuse me, Jed," Mrs. Wigglesworth replied, looking down her long, bumpy nose at him (she was a member of the original Longnose founding family on her mother's side), "but taking turns is what counts. Being fair to all."

"What's so fair about losing?" Marco grumbled. "That's unfair to us."

"Excuse me, Mrs. Wigglesworth. I just want to say something. Isabella never takes turns," Nicky said. "She's a major swing hogger. And she does it on purpose. Her motto is—"

"Yeah! We all know her motto, don't we, guys?" called out Jimmy from the back. "On the count of three, everybody. One, two, three!"

"I won't share 'cuz it's not fair!" Nicky, Marco, Jimmy, and Jed shouted in unison.

The class was utterly silent. Kids looked at one another as if to say, Could that *really* be her motto? Did Isabella really refuse to share?

"Her name should be Isabella Swinghogger," Nicky said.

"Yeah. Or Isabella Poolhogger," added Marco, glaring at her.

Isabella hung her head in shame. Mrs. Wigglesworth simply stared at her. A child who refused to share?

Finally Mrs. Wigglesworth said, "Nevertheless, my decision is final. Isabella Speedwalker-Juarez is our pitcher. I'm sure she'll do us proud."

7

Deborah glanced at Isabella and gave her a little smile of sympathy. Isabella looked down at her lap. Her cheeks were scarlet. She hadn't even been at this school for one whole morning. She hadn't realized how much her motto might truly bother other kids. She'd thought it was a good idea for herself—because of the tiny bedroom and everything.

But never mind her motto. Now she got to be pitcher? How exciting! She had never, ever been pitcher in kickball. She'd hardly ever played kickball. Her specialty was soccer. And now her turn to be the star had come. She just couldn't give it up.

"Spelling time. Take out your spelling workbooks. Turn to page 162 and remember, neatness counts, boys and girls."

When Mrs. Wigglesworth went back to the blackboard, Jed leaned over and whispered, "Isabelly. Doesn't share the bread and jelly."

"Shut up!" Isabella whispered desperately. "Please."

"No," said Marco, beaming. "Not till you give up pitching for us."

In total frustration, Isabella raised her hand. "Mrs. Wigglesworth? Jed and Marco are calling me names. They're calling me Isabelly and I don't like it."

Mrs. Wigglesworth whirled around. "Jed? Marco? What seems to be the problem?"

"We won't win the kickball game if Isabella pitches," Marco said.

"Yeah," said Jed.

"But this is a great chance for me. I've never, ever been a pitcher in kickball before," Isabella said.

Jed and Marco groaned. "See? She has no experience at all," said Jed.

"So you decided to call her names?" demanded Mrs. Wigglesworth. "You know how I feel about name-calling. I simply cannot allow it."

"Well, yes," Marco admitted. "I did make up a name, so I guess I started it. I told Jed that nickname earlier." He got up and wrote his name on the board under a small sign that said NO RECESS TODAY.

"Thank you, Marco. Now, how is it, Jed, that you think you should represent our class in kickball? Someone who behaves badly when my back is turned? Why shouldn't our new student have the privilege of being pitcher?"

By this time, Isabella was feeling terrible. She had told on the boys and broken the kids' sacred code of honor. She'd had no idea they would get into so

47

much trouble. She wished Mrs. Wigglesworth would stop talking about it. She glanced across her desk and whispered, "Sorry, Marco."

He nodded. "That's okay," he whispered back.

Nicky, whose desk was beside hers, gave her a quick pat on the back. He must know how bad she was feeling.

Isabella remembered that she'd snatched the swing from him earlier. Nicky was pretty nice. What on earth was wrong with her?

Isabella stared at her spelling words: "finally," "forever," and "friends." She felt so embarrassed and confused that she thought she might cry. Quickly she got up and asked Mrs. Wigglesworth if she could go to the girls' room. She speedwalked down the hall to the pink-tiled bathroom.

She took some paper towels, wet them, and wiped the tear streaks from her face with cool water. She cleared her throat a few times.

There. That was better. She was in a tough situation, no doubt about it, but her life would quickly become a lot tougher if she missed spelling and cursive by hiding out in the girls' room. She had to go back. Those boys were just a bunch of teases. They didn't really hate her. At least, Nicky and Marco didn't. She wasn't sure about Jed.

• • •

The day dragged on. Fortunately, Deborah stuck by Isabella all the way through. When the girls got home, Deborah even invited her over for a snack.

"No, thanks," Isabella said. "I'm really tired. I think I'll rest for a little while before Dozer gets home from day care."

"Sure. See you later."

"Bye. And thanks for everything."

Isabella pushed open the front door. Granny was in the salon soaking a group of black-bristled hairbrushes in a plastic container of bleach. The odor nipped at the inside of Isabella's nose. She heard a timer ding.

"Hi, Granny."

"Hello, dear. Go on in the kitchen. Cookies are in the jar. Take one. I'm busy right now."

Granny was in the middle of giving a perm. The timer going off meant she had to rinse the chemicals out of her customer's hair.

Isabella grabbed a cookie and hurried to her room. She waded through the wadded-up clothes on the floor, pushed her crayons and coloring books to one side with her sneaker, and pulled her favorite armadillo, the pink one, from the mess in the closet before climbing onto the top bunk.

She stared at the ceiling, which seemed only inches from her nose. How awful her day had been.

How could she be the third-grade pitcher? Pitching in kickball was sort of like bowling. She'd never been bowling. She'd better practice like crazy.

And telling on those boys! She'd been teased about her name before. Big deal. It was all because of her motto, her not-sharing motto. That was making the kids mad. That was what had shocked the teacher.

She couldn't just lie around like a bunk-bed potato. She climbed down from the bunk, dug around in her closet for her soccer ball, pulled off the sign that was taped to her bedroom door, and made a beeline for Zach's fix-it shop. Maybe he could fix whatever it was that was wrong with her.

8

Zach was testing the big green riding mower, riding it around and around the yard, so Isabella had to wait for nearly fifteen minutes with nothing to do but bounce the soccer ball on her forehead till she got a headache. Then he circled the garage once more and stopped beside her.

"Hey, Isabella. How was school?"

"Okay. Sort of."

"Just okay?"

"Terrible, actually. I was kind of a jerk."

"I guess we can all be jerks, one way or another." Zach laughed.

And then Isabella laughed. She thought of herself trying to snatch the swing from Nicky. Being late to class. Telling on Jed and Marco. Good grief!

"Going to start your car wash business today? Good weather for it," Zach said.

"Maybe. Look. I brought you my motto. I think it needs fixing." She handed him the sign. "I wanted to have a motto like you do. Mine is about not sharing. Sharing means you have to wait. It means you never get what you want. You always have to give to other people. Why? Why can't they watch out for themselves? Anyway, at school, I wouldn't share the swing today. And I wouldn't give up being kickball pitcher, even though I don't know how to do it. Now everyone's mad at me."

Zach rubbed his chin thoughtfully. Finally he tacked the paper up on the wall of the garage and stared at it. "So this is causing you some problems?" he said.

"Well, yeah. But I don't really get it. Giving means you have less, right?" said Isabella.

"No. It might seem that way at first. But, no, giving makes you richer. I think butting heads with you about this is not going to work, so . . ." He was silent for a moment. "You know, I'd like to help you with that car wash. How about I make a plywood sign for it."

"Really! You'd do that?"

"Sure. Nothing to it. Just nail two braces on the back and you can stand the sign up at the street corner whenever you're open for business. You won't be able to lift it. Plywood is plenty heavy. You can pull it down there with Dozer's wagon," Zach added.

"I'll go ask him."

Isabella dashed home and found a very tired little

Dozer, just home from day care, sprawled in front of the TV with a bottle of juice. Her mom was in the kitchen, unloading groceries.

"Hey, Dozer, can I borrow your wagon? I need it to move my car wash sign."

"No."

"But you're not using it. I just want to borrow it for a minute."

"No, Belly. Mine. My wagon."

"I'm gonna take it. I'll bring it right back."

"No, Belly, mine!" Dozer began to howl.

Granny hurried in from the salon. "Now what?"

"Nothing. I just want to borrow his wagon is all."

"You? Aren't you the one who put these goldurned signs up about not sharing? You better do without borrowing anybody's anything, don't you think? Come here, Dozer. Come to Granny. Joann? Let's go find your mommy, okay, sweetie?"

Everyone took his side because he was little.

Moping, Isabella dragged herself back to Zach's yard. "He says I can't use the wagon," she reported.

"I see," Zach said. "A set of wheels would have been a big help. Did you offer him a ride in the wagon after you got done? That might have softened him up a bit."

"No." She hadn't even thought of it. Maybe she

54

should rethink this not-sharing business in terms of trade-offs. But right now she preferred to sulk.

Isabella watched as Zach painted the whole side of a three-foot-by-three-foot piece of exterior-grade plywood white and then cut two two-by-fours for braces. She helped nail them in place. Zach let her use his eight-ounce hammer. He said the sixteen-ounce one was lethal.

He set the board in the sun. In twenty minutes it was dry. Then he drew the outlines of the letters for her and she painted them in with red paint. It was a pretty messy business. And rinsing the paintbrushes afterward seemed to take an hour. Getting the paint off Isabella's hands, hair, and face took a long time, too. But in the end, the sign was beautiful. It read:

ISABELLA'S CAR WASH AT ZACH'S FIX-IT SHOP
STOP BY REAL SOON

"To do business in a small town like Center Long-nose, you need to keep on good terms with every-body. You want your customers to feel welcome and sure that you're going to do right by them."

"But guess what. I don't have polite-type manners," Isabella said.

"What you do have is a lot of enthusiasm. You're full of ideas. That's great. Really, Izzy, that's a gift."

Zach was a very good friend, Isabella thought. She wished he would pat her head, but maybe they didn't know each other well enough for that. She thought about her new idea of trade-offs. Zach had painted the sign. What could she offer in return? Right away she had an idea.

"Dozer's birthday is Saturday. Think you can come to the party?" she asked.

Zach suddenly looked bashful. "Saturday? He'll be three years old? So would your dad be coming to this party?"

"No. My mom and dad are divorced. He lives in California. With a circus lady. An acrobat. She twirls by her hair on a rope."

"If he won't be there, I guess I'll come, then."

Isabella wanted to invite Deborah, too. And it would be fun giving Dozer the little pool. That way, when the big pool came, he would already have his own. And she wouldn't have to share her great big pool with a three-year-old.

Granny had cooked dinner, but it was Isabella's job to set the table and her mom's to clear it and load the dishwasher. They were going to have pork chops, applesauce, and lima beans. Isabella did not like lima beans. Maybe she could talk to Granny about it.

"Granny, can I have something else instead of those beans?"

"Nope. This isn't a restaurant."

"But I like carrots. I could eat a carrot in place of the beans."

"Nope."

Isabella frowned and folded her arms in a hug. Granny was being unfair. On the other hand, Isabella could see that Granny had worked hard all day and wasn't used to feeding three extra people. Maybe it was too hard for her to fuss with carrots now.

"How did school go today, Isabella?" her mom asked quickly. She handed Isabella a handful of silverware.

"All right. I'm going to be kickball pitcher at the annual third-and-fourth-grade game at the end of the month."

"Great! But since when are you good at that?"

"I don't know. I was never picked for pitcher before."

"I bet it's a lot like bowling," Granny said. "I was the Longnose Bowling Queen in 1976. The Baddeals used to run the bowling alley. Overcharged everybody then, too."

"I've never bowled," Isabella replied. "Can I practice pitching with you, Mom?"

Her mother sighed. "Sure. Sometime." She sank into a chair at the table.

"What's wrong, Mom?"

"Oh, things at the factory aren't looking too good."

"Don't you worry about earning that pool money," said Isabella. "Once my car wash gets under way, we are going to be all set. Zach and I made a big plywood sign for the car wash. A huge one, bigger than Dozer. And Deborah and I put up two ads at the end of the street."

As the family sat down to dinner, Isabella's mom said, "The truth is, the factory is in danger of closing altogether unless we come up with a new product. We really need a flavor nobody else has. The research director is holding a contest for a new idea. The winner gets two hundred dollars."

Isabella's eyebrows leaped into two surprised arches. "Ho, ho! Did you say two hundred dollars?" she asked.

"Yep."

"Yowee kazowee." Isabella began to boogie in her seat. "Just in the nick of time."

"It's not so easy to do," her mother said. "Watermelon was an easy flavor, but we developed a watermelon-flavored gum a long time ago. And orange was easy, too. So were the mints, and cinnamon, and licorice. But other gum companies have those flavors also. Longnose Gum needs something different to distinguish it."

"Isabella, eat your lima beans," said Granny.

"Do I have to? I tried one but I really do hate lima beans." Isabella was plumb out of sympathy for Granny.

"Me too," said Dozer. "Hate lima beans."

Granny looked at Isabella. "Well, all right. Since you tried one. Guess I'm not used to sharing my house, either. Why don't you go ahead and peel yourself a carrot. Is that a good deal?"

Isabella gave Granny the thumbs-up. "Yep."

Her mother continued, "So anyway, if the gum factory closes, we may have to move to a larger town, like Lubbock or Abilene. There's no other work here in Longnose except at the grain depot or the train yard."

"Move again? We just got here, for Pete's sake. No more moving!" said Isabella. But maybe if they moved, she could have her own room. Maybe there would be a soccer team to join. Still, it was funny, but already she knew she would miss Deborah and Zach and maybe even Nicky. What a mix-up she was inside.

"Now, this weekend is Dozer's birthday," Isabella's mother said. "We'll have his party about one-thirty on Saturday."

"With cupcakes. And cherry punch. And I invited Zach already."

Isabella's mom smiled. "Well, that was nice." Isabella wondered if her mom liked Zach. Maybe they would go out together sometime.

"Granny, seems like your car is all dusty. My car wash only costs two dollars."

"As long as I don't have to wash it." Granny winked at Isabella. "Because I sure am tired. Whoooeee. My back aches. My dogs are sore tonight," said Granny, pushing her chair away from the table. "Too many customers today."

Granny always called her feet her dogs when they hurt.

"Maybe I'll have to take up hairdressing as well, if I lose my job at the factory," said Isabella's mom.

"Oh no you don't. More hairdressers will put me out of business. Besides, how are people going to pay for a new hairdo if the factory closes down?" Granny asked.

Not even the talk about Dozer's birthday helped. Because of the problems at the gum factory, the atmosphere at the dinner table was getting decidedly glum. Isabella ate her carrot, then excused herself and cleared her plate. "Thanks for dinner, Granny," she said. Well, for most of it, she thought.

Isabella sat in her room with her stuffed toys. She picked up her favorite pink armadillo. "Hey, Dillie, listen to this! If I can invent a new flavored gum, I'll win the two hundred dollars, and the pool will be ours. Course, I might have to wash a few cars, too, in case there are extra expenses. Or in case we come in second in the gum-flavor contest. Now, let's see. This shouldn't be hard. Dillie, did you say, 'How about scrambled-egg gum'?"

She tried to imagine it. Would it be yellow like the yolk? Gooey? With crackly brown edges? Somehow she couldn't picture it. "No, Dillie. That's no good. Kids don't like eggs much anyway. What do they like?"

Fruits were finished. Mints overused. Maybe . . . maybe pizza gum! Tomato-flavored gum seemed okay, but what about the cheese part?

"That's no good either, Dillie. Cheese and gum do not go together. Cheese smells weird most of the time. Don't you think so? You have a great big snout. How does cheese smell to you? Bad? I thought so. Well, what, then?"

Isabella climbed onto her bed, raised the screen,

and crawled feet first out the window. She dropped to the ground. With Dillie tucked under her arm, she crossed the backyard to the sycamore tree. It would be nice to have a swing.

Zach could probably make Isabella a tire swing in no time flat. He had piles of old tires behind the fix-it shop.

Isabella lay down on her back in the dirt and propped Dillie on her stomach. Overhead the stars came out like teeny blue flowers popping open. She tried to think about the gum flavor. It had to be something kids really liked. Chocolate! That was her favorite! But there was already so much chocolate candy available.

What else did kids really like? And then she had it. Peanut butter. Peanut-butter gum. What a great idea. She'd make some and try it out. She knew Deborah would want to help her.

9

A few days later, Deborah and Isabella sat on the floor of Isabella and Dozer's room, madly chewing piece after piece of Longnose tutti-frutti chewing gum to get the flavor out of it. When the gum was completely tasteless, they dropped that piece in a jar and started on the next.

"My jaws hurt," said Deborah. "And we'll probably get cavities."

"Nope. I bought sugarless gum, of course."

Finally they'd chewed all the gum. Now they had to mix in the peanut butter. From the kitchen cupboard, Isabella took out a bowl and put a big blob of peanut butter in the bottom. Deborah dumped in some chewed gum. They tried to stir it together, but the stiff gum didn't mix easily with the crunchy peanut butter.

"Oh, no!" said Isabella. "This has to work! It has to!"

"I know. Let's start over. Just take some gum and chew the flavor out. Then add whatever kind of flavor you want right in your mouth!" Deborah said.

"Wow! Yeah. Then you can make it as peanut

buttery as you want. Like designer gum. Let's draw a diagram, too."

They showed the sketches to Isabella's mom.

She laughed. "Brilliant!" she said. "Kids today are so smart."

"Smarter than kids yesterday?" Isabella teased. "And the day before?"

"Yep. I'll take the drawings into the lab for you, if you want," she said. "Put your names on the back. I don't think they really want samples of already-chewed gum."

"Okay. Hey! Do you think we'll win?" Isabella asked.

"I do. Now, bedtime. Deborah needs to head home. And Izzy needs to head to the tub."

"See you tomorrow," said Isabella, grinning.

"Good night," Deborah said.

Saturday, April 8, was the day of Dozer's third birthday party, and Isabella's chore was to help clean the house. Granny put the ancient vacuum cleaner, its hose patched with duct tape, in her hands.

"Do I have to, Granny? Dozer doesn't care if the rug is vacuumed. Can't I go outside? Please?" she begged. Isabella felt her activity level building to a peak.

"Your cousins are coming. Zach is coming. I want the house spick-and-span."

"I don't care about that."

"Well, I care," her grandmother said. "Now start hoovering, girl."

Isabella smiled as she switched on the motor. Hoover was the brand name of the vacuum cleaner.

In the kitchen, her mom was making the cherry cupcakes. And Dozer was sitting in his empty plastic pool out back, waiting for water. Isabella had promised to hook up Zach's hose and fill the pool for him as soon as she finished vacuuming.

Isabella hoovered around just as fast as she could. She liked it when she hit patches of real dirt. She liked the little rattly noise the dirt made as it was sucked up through the metal tube into the canister.

Just as she finished and wound up the cord, the phone rang. "I'll get it! Oh, hello, Auntie Florence. What? You're not coming? Mom, the cousins aren't coming! Why not? Oh. Bad weather this afternoon. Really? Mom, they're not coming because there's going to be some whopper thunderstorms this afternoon. Hail and lightning and stuff."

"Oh, for heaven's sake," her mother said.

"Guess what, Auntie Florence, I just had to hoover the rug for you guys and now you tell me you're not coming. You should have said so beforehand. Dozer got a plastic pool. Yeah, he likes it. All right, now. You take care, too. Say hi to everybody."

Isabella hung up. "How do you like that?"

"Party poopers," her mother said, putting the cupcakes into the oven to bake.

"Belly! Help me!" Dozer called. "I need water! Pool needs water."

"All right, birthday boy."

She dragged the hose over the fence from Zach's fix-it shop.

"You need help with that, Isabella?" Zach asked.

"No, thanks. I got it. Now, Dozer, here we go!"

She held the nozzle up in the air so that it sprayed like a fountain. The soft mist of water felt delightful on her hot cheeks and forehead. When the pool was filled to about eight inches deep, she dragged the hose back to the fix-it shop.

"Some nasty puffy clouds are piling up to the south of here," said Zach. "Take a look."

"You think it's going to rain on the party? My aunt and cousins aren't even going to come on account of the weather forecast."

"Well, I'll be there. I guess there will be more cake for me, then."

"Yeah!" They wouldn't have to share the cupcakes with her four cousins. "You can't fool me, Zach. Sometimes you like not sharing, too!" Isabella laughed.

"You know what? I hate to admit it, but you're right!"

The party got started about two o'clock. There were balloons tied to the fence posts. Deborah and her parents came. Zach lugged his picnic table over for everyone to sit at. And Dozer's buddy from day care showed up with his mom. The two little kids sat in the pool and splashed each other, laughing with delight.

Isabella watched them wistfully. "When I get my pool, we can play for hours like those two," she said to Deborah.

"I can't wait! I hope we win that gum-flavor contest."

"Criminy. That sky is getting awfully dark," Deborah's mom said.

"Look at those purple clouds!" Isabella said, biting into the cherry icing on her cupcake. Isabella always ate her icing first. "Hey! Look! Lightning!"

Crack! Bam! Booom!

And then came the rain—torrents of rain. Everyone shrieked and ran for cover. The guests headed for their car. Deborah and her mom dashed across the street. And Zach and the Speedwalker-Juarez family hurried inside. The party was over.

Crash! Flash! Booom! Thunder was okay. But Isabella was terrified of lightning. It looked like the sky was ripping. So she went to sit in her closet with Dillie. Dillie didn't mind thunderstorms. She was covered with a thick pink plush hide.

It was nice and dark in the closet, but it was awfully stuffy. Isabella hoped the storm wouldn't last long because she had the door closed tightly. And then all of a sudden, above the rattle of the lashing rain, she heard an enormous rumble that sounded as if a freight train were coming up the driveway.

"Hey, Dillie. Do you hear that great, big, grumbly noise? Don't be scared now. Mom? Mom?" she called.

The trailer began to shake. The train noise grew deafening. "Mom? Help! I'm scared!" Isabella yelled in a panic. But she realized no one could possibly hear her above the roar.

This was no train. It had to be a twister. And they didn't even have a basement to hide in. She pulled tightly on the doorknob to hold it shut in case the roof got sucked off.

"Ohhhh," she muttered. "Please, God, make everyone be safe. Please. Please. Please! Make everyone be safe. I promise I'll share stuff. I will, really I will. I won't be bossy or selfish or a bad influence ever, ever again."

Then, abruptly, it was over. There was silence.

10

Isabella opened the closet door and looked up. She didn't see sky. The roof was still on. The bedroom was okay. Thank God.

"Mom!" she screamed, scrambling to her feet. "Where are you?"

"Here! In the kitchen. Are you okay, Isabella?"

Isabella looked around the room. All her pictures had blown off the walls. The tissues had been sucked out of the box and were plastered against the screens in the windows in soggy pastel lumps. But basically, their precious room was all right.

Isabella yanked open the bedroom door and ran down the hall. "Mom, are you guys okay?"

Granny, her mother, and Zach were just crawling out from under the kitchen table. The kitchen had barely been touched.

Her mother hugged her tightly.

"I hid in my closet with the door closed! The tissues were all sucked out of the box!"

"Hooooeee! I bet that tornado touched down awful close by," Zach said. "What a racket!"

71

"Uh-oh. Where's Dozer?" Isabella asked in a panicky voice.

Granny pointed. "Under there."

Sure enough, Dozer was curled up asleep under the kitchen table.

"He slept through a tornado!" Isabella said.

"Isn't he a sound sleeper?" Granny asked proudly. "That's my Dozer."

"Whoa. Hooey. Take a look out here, Isabella," said Zach, standing at the back door, shaking his head in amazement. "Isn't life something? Isn't it something?"

Dozer's pool was up in the sycamore tree, stuck in the branches. And Zach's fix-it shop was nothing but a pile of rubble.

"Your shop! It's been blown to bits!" Isabella cried out.

He nodded, evidently unable to speak for a second. Finally he said, "Incredible. I guess the twister touched down once and then bounced on out of here. I'm glad we're safe, Isabella. That old shop doesn't matter. Just some nails and boards banged together. I told you walls don't matter, right?"

Isabella started to cry. She felt terrible that Zach's shop had been destroyed. "I'm really sorry that happened to you, Zach," she said. "It isn't fair at all. The whole neighborhood looks mostly like it's okay. Just your shop is wrecked."

"Hey, hey. It's all right. We're okay. I can get some more boards. And as for my shop being the only wreck, that's how it goes with tornadoes. You don't know what they'll ruin and what they won't. I can build another one. Don't worry about it, Isabella. Who ever said life is fair, anyway?"

Then they all had a glass of cherry punch to celebrate surviving the twister on Dozer's third birthday—all except Dozer, who continued sleeping.

The next day, Sunday, it seemed as if everyone in Center Longnose was up and out, walking around, talking about the storm. A little after nine, Isabella loaded the plywood sign onto Dozer's wagon, and with Dozer pushing from the back and Deborah pulling from the front and Isabella steadying the large board, they pulled it down to the corner and propped it upright.

They stood back to survey their handiwork. Dozer climbed into the wagon for his promised ride home.

"There, Dozer. Looks good, doesn't it? Thanks for helping me out," said Isabella. "Anybody who can't see that sign is blind as a bat."

"Are bats really blind?" Deborah asked. "They have eyes, you know."

"They do? Okay. Anyone who can't see that is

blind as a bat with his eyes shut. Now come on, let's go hook up the hoses."

Isabella ran back down their road, pulling the rattly wagon behind her. Dozer clutched the sides. "Faster, Belly. Faster!" he crowed. "Hee, hee."

"He's so cute," Deborah said.

"Yeah, mostly."

"Listen. I bet everyone's cars got splattered with mud from the tornado. We don't have a moment to lose. I'll get some buckets and some detergent," Deborah said. "Be right back!"

"We need a box to put the money in," Isabella said.

"Okay! I'll get one." Deborah dashed into her house.

Then, as Isabella raced up the driveway, still pulling the wagon, she realized she might have a big problem. The hoses had been in Zach's garage. And the garage was nothing but a heap of boards, broken glass, sticking-up nails, tools, and muddy rainwater.

"Hey, howdy," Zach said, coming out with his morning cup of coffee.

"I was looking for those hoses, Zach," Isabella said in a small voice. "But maybe they were ruined. I forgot for a moment your shop was wrecked so badly."

"Yeah." He sighed. "Guess I'll have to fix my own fix-it shop." He gave her a wink.

"Zach, do you think the hoses are okay?"

He pulled on two heavy work gloves. "There's only one way to find out."

Zach began pulling boards out of the wreckage and tossing them into a heap. The hoses were perfectly fine, if a little muddy.

Isabella and Deborah got their buckets and sponges and sat down beside the road in lawn chairs. They waited for two hours, but not one single car came down their street to be washed.

"You know, even though the cars are dirty, maybe no one's thinking about washing them today," Deborah suggested.

"Could be. We need a hundred cars to earn enough money. I bet at this rate we don't get a single one. Well, we can do Granny's."

"And my mother's. So that's two."

"Hey! Look. There's Marco and Nicky. On their bikes!"

They circled closer and closer, like a pair of sharks, around the end of Zach's driveway. "Guess what, guys! You won't believe it," Nicky said. "Jimmy Pettifogger's roof got sucked off by the twister. He lives two streets over. Come on. We'll show you."

Deborah and Isabella ran for their bikes. Zach offered to keep an eye out for customers while they went to check out the storm damage.

Tree branches, huge ones, were down all over Center Longnose. So just about everyone had to get their chainsaws out, oil them up, and cut wood this Sunday morning. The buzzing and whirring noise was tremendous. Fortunately, the downed wires had been cleared aside and carefully marked.

As the children rode over to Jimmy's, they passed a fire hydrant that had popped loose, spraying water all over the place. It was fun to ride their bikes through the huge puddle. They each took a couple of turns sending a V-shaped wedge of water out on either side of their bikes. Then they headed off to Jimmy's street nearby.

His street was a mess of debris, with branches down, litter everywhere, windows broken, and every single thing spattered with globs of mud. But the only house that was actually damaged was the Pettifoggers' one-story ranch down at the end. The tornado had ripped off Jimmy Pettifogger's roof. It was completely gone—half the chimney, too.

Isabella, Deborah, Nicky, and Marco stared in awe as Jimmy told them the whole scary story, how his entire family had been squashed down inside the bathtub, holding on to the faucets for dear life, and how he saw the towels and the toilet paper get sucked up into the air, which was swirling above his house at about two hundred miles an hour.

"Come on. I'll give you the tour," he said. "My room is such a huge mess." His eyes filled with tears, and he blinked them back. "But we'll fix it. You'll see."

The kids peeked through a hole in the wall. They could see that Jimmy's bedroom was almost completely destroyed. The pictures had been knocked off the walls, the closet door had been ripped off and was sticking out through a window, the dresser had toppled onto the bed. Clothes and soggy blankets and toys were scattered everywhere, and everything was covered with sprays of mud.

"Wow," Marco said.

"Criminy," said Isabella. She'd never seen anything like it before.

"And you were all in the bathtub, Jimmy?" Deborah asked. "The whole family?"

"Plus the dog. We were all in there. The walls and tub came through without a scratch."

"Weren't you scared?" asked Nicky.

"Yep. Scared to death."

Isabella, Nicky, Deborah, and Marco walked back to their bikes. Jimmy's mother led him across the street to the neighbors' house, where they were staying for now.

"His toys are wrecked. He needs help," Nicky said in a low voice.

"I know! How about using the car wash to help

him?" Deborah said to Isabella excitedly. "We can wash cars today and earn some money for Jimmy to buy some new toys."

"Yeah," the boys said together.

"Isabella?" Deborah asked. "Is that okay?"

Oh, no! She felt confused. Of course she wanted to help Jimmy. His bedroom problem was much, much, much worse than hers! How could she even think of herself at a time like this? But sharing still didn't come easily to Isabella, and she hesitated. If she said no, then none of her new friends, including Zach, would understand. And she would be ashamed of herself for not doing better when she had promised she absolutely would during the twister.

"Yeah. Okay. Yeah, we can give him some money. That's a great idea," she said slowly.

"I know you wanted it for your pool," Deborah said softly, "but there's still the gum-flavor contest."

Isabella nodded miserably.

"Besides that big car wash sign you guys made, we'll also have me and Nicky out yelling at cars as they go by and explaining about the Pettifoggers. Then you girls can wash the cars down at Zach's and take donations."

But what about the pool money? What if they didn't win the gum contest? Isabella wondered as she rode back to Zach's house behind the others. She didn't even have fun riding through the huge puddle and gave up her second turn to Nicky.

With Nicky and Marco out on the main street, hooting and hollering about raising money for the Pettifoggers, the car wash was a huge success. Together, the four of them washed a hundred cars. Well, Zach did a lot of work, too. And so did Isabella's mom. And Granny ended up being in charge of the little cash box. They all celebrated afterward with homemade pepperoni pizza and lemonade.

They had made two hundred dollars, all in single-dollar bills. Granny put rubber bands around them in groups of twenty—ten groups.

"Two hundred smackeroos," Isabella said. "Think we should take it over to him now?"

"I think someone had better go with you," her mom said.

Deborah, Isabella's mother, and Isabella walked over to Jimmy's neighbors' house, while Nicky and Marco rode their bikes. The kids proudly presented Jimmy with the money. His mother cried and his dad's nose was red. Isabella thought that maybe he was crying a little, too. They seemed touched that Jimmy's classmates had worked so hard to help.

Walking back, Deborah and Isabella were very quiet. It was going to be hard for the Pettifoggers to rebuild their lives, and it would take a long time.

Isabella felt she had been acting like a big baby, sulking about having to live at her granny's trailer, when really it was easy to see how lucky they were to have one another.

"Good night, sweetie," her mother said as she tucked Isabella tightly into her bunk. "I'm very proud of what you kids did today."

"I helped, too," said Dozer from down below.

"What? Oh, yeah. You shared your wagon. That's right," Isabella said.

"That was really very generous of you, Isabella."

"Yeah, Mom, but you know what? I had to try very, very hard to be glad that we gave Jimmy such a big gift. And I'm trying very, very hard not to be sad that we didn't keep any money for the pool fund." A few tears escaped from the corners of Isabella's eyes, and she brushed them away.

"I know," her mother said, kissing her. "It's okay to have such mixed-up feelings. You gave up a lot when you gave Jimmy that money. Maybe you'll get a call soon from Mr. Wigglesworth about your peanut-butter gum."

"Maybe, but, well, there's no point in getting my hopes up," Isabella said.

"Oh, sweetie. Yes, there is. You go on and get your hopes up! Now, nighty-night, Izzy."

"Nighty-night."

11

While Isabella waited to hear from Mr. Wigglesworth, she thought maybe she should try to run the car wash again. But she also had to practice pitching for the upcoming game. She couldn't let her classmates down. She had to at least try to do her best.

So every day after school, instead of washing cars, she got out her soccer ball and practiced for speed and accuracy. She rolled it at a pile of empty Gatorade bottles, a heap of her armadillos, a stack of old inner tubes, even at the trunk of the sycamore tree. Every pitch seemed to be off.

Deborah watched. "Too slow, Izzy. Outside. Faster!"

When things got really bad, Isabella took to heading the ball from her forehead. That she was good at. "Maybe I can lob it at them like this," she said.

"I don't think you're allowed to pitch that way in kickball," Deborah answered.

Taking into account the insurance money he'd been promised, Zach bought a whole stack of lumber, bags of nails, hundreds of pounds of cement mix, and asphalt roofing tiles for his new shop. "I'm planning on making this shop bigger and sturdier than the old one," he told Isabella one day.

"Big is good. Texas-big. Maybe we can put a bowling alley in it."

Zach stared at her.

"Just kidding." She grinned.

Soon two weeks had gone by, and the Pettifoggers already had their new roof. If the Speedwalker-Juarezes didn't have *their* two hundred dollars in eight more days, the pool would be lost. And still the people at the Longnose Gum factory hadn't said a word about Isabella's new idea.

After school on Monday, April 24, Isabella picked up her eight-ounce hammer, and she and Zach were hammering together the forms to hold the new concrete floor when Deborah arrived. "Hey! I heard all that banging clear across the street. I thought we were practicing kickball today. It's just two more days till the game."

"Nah. I think I'm in pretty good shape now. Besides, I gotta help my buddy here," Isabella said. "First things first." At this point, she far preferred construction to pitching. Despite all her practice, she still worried that her pitching might cause her class to lose the game.

"You can help us, Deborah," said Zach. "But I'm fresh out of hammers. You'll have to go get your own."

Deborah dashed home and was back in minutes to take her place alongside Isabella.

Before long, they got one wall studded up and the plywood nailed on. Then they took a short break. Isabella's palm was beet-red from holding the hammer. Her whole hand felt as if it were vibrating from the repeated banging.

"Let me see your hands. You kids don't want to be getting blisters," said Zach. "I'm ordering you to play for the rest of the afternoon."

So Isabella and Deborah got out the ball again. Isabella practiced pitching; Deborah kicked, or tried to. Then they switched places.

Isabella wasn't spectacular as pitcher, but, wow, could she kick! She booted the ball high into the air, time after time.

"You have such strong legs, even if they are skinny," Deborah said. "And you can aim that ball wherever."

"It's because I'm a Speedwalker-Juarez. All that speedwalking pays off, I guess."

After she'd finished dinner and her math homework, Isabella wandered outside and climbed the fence. Zach was working under a couple of floodlights he'd rigged up. He wanted to finish pouring the concrete floor tonight, it seemed to Isabella as she watched. He had just poured the final batch of smooth, gooey gray cement at what would be the new shop entrance.

"Go get Dozer, Izzy. You can put your handprints and footprints in the wet cement, just like the stars do in Hollywood. Go on, now."

Afterward, Isabella sat admiring her prints. She scratched the date beside them.

"Next year, when you're grown a bit," said Zach, "you'll look back and think how small you used to be. Specially you, Dozer."

"Zach!" said Isabella suddenly. "Even though he hasn't called me, I'm going to get in touch with Mr. Wigglesworth about my new gum flavor. I have to win that two hundred dollars."

"A new gum flavor? Wow. Can I try a piece?" Zach took the hose and rinsed the cement off his shovel.

"I don't think so. I don't want anyone to find out about it ahead of time."

"I see. Pretty sure you've got a winner there, are you?"

"Yep. But I guess you can have a test piece. Just you, and only as long as you don't tell Nicky and Marco."

Zach gave her a look that said, What kind of dummy do you think I am anyway, and Isabella sped off to get some fresh gum and a jar of peanut butter.

She came flying back. Zach unwrapped the gum and popped it into his mouth to chew the flavor out. Then he took a spoonful of peanut butter, just as Isabella directed him. He chewed thoughtfully for a moment and then nodded. "Yessiree. You've got something here. Kind of crunchy. Different. Not fruity at all."

Isabella danced and twirled in circles. And then she said, "Hey, Zach? Can you make me a tire swing way up high in the sycamore so no one else can get on it?"

"No."

Isabella stopped twirling and looked at him. Then she asked, "Can you make me a tire swing, please? If I let other kids use it, too?"

"Of course," he said. "I'll do it tonight."

"Hooray! Thanks, Zach!" She hopped up and down like a pogo stick gone berserk.

"Isabella!" called her mother. "Bedtime!"

"Grr. Why does she have to yell bedtime so the whole neighborhood can hear?" Isabella grumbled.

Zach laughed. "See you later, Izzy-gator."

"Yeah, later, Zach."

As she climbed over the fence, she thought what

a good friend Zach was and how generous, how he shared whatever he had: boards, nails, hammers, an old tire, or just plain time and good ideas, ideas that seemed almost as if she'd thought them up herself. That was the best part. She'd tell Dillie all about it when she went to bed.

12

Tuesday arrived. Isabella had decided to go down to the Longnose Gum factory and talk to Mr. Wigglesworth herself. He'd had plenty of time to choose the contest winner.

Before doing anything else, Isabella dashed to the bathroom window and looked out at the sycamore tree. There, from the lowest branch, hung the tire swing Zach had promised. Isabella smiled. What a peach he was.

The hours at school went slowly by. Finally the three o'clock bell rang. Isabella and Deborah hurried all the way home. Isabella changed her clothes and dashed out to meet Deborah in the driveway. Both girls were wearing dresses and shiny party shoes with straps across the tops of the feet.

"Hey, you look nice," Deborah said.

"Yeah. You too. But I hope Nicky and Marco don't see us all fancied up like this."

The front door slammed. Isabella's mom had taken the afternoon off, since the gum-factory workers were being encouraged to take plenty of unpaid flextime. She came down the walk, digging around in her purse for the car keys. She was wearing her plastic click-clack sandals, which Isabella knew meant that her mother was in no mood for frivolity.

"Hop into the car, ladies," she said, her voice determined and businesslike. "We're off."

Her mother was probably fretting about being home on a Tuesday afternoon, instead of being allowed to work and earn money.

They drove in silence to the factory, a long, dull building painted light gray, the color of dryer lint. A row of almost-useless windows stretched along the front, too high for kids to peek into.

As they hurried up the sidewalk past the flagpole and its bed of straggly bluebonnets, Deborah said in a low voice, "I'm getting nervous."

"Me too," whispered Isabella. "Maybe they hate our idea and that's why they didn't call."

"This way," her mother said as she ushered them through the front door and down the hall to the right. Suddenly a loud buzzer went off. Deborah jumped. "Oh! What was that?"

"That means there's a shift change on the factory floor."

"This place is kind of like a school," Isabella said.

"Yes. In some ways. Now, here's the manager's office. Don't be nervous, girls. He's very nice. And very fair. Well, he *is* a Wigglesworth."

"Nice to meet you, Mr. Wigglesworth," Isabella said, practicing. "I guess we're all set," she added.

"All right," said her mother. "I'll wait for you right outside the front door. Good luck, girls."

Deborah tugged at Isabella's hand. "I can't do this," she whispered.

"You can't poop out on me now, Deborah!" Isabella whispered back.

"Ladies?" Mr. Wigglesworth's secretary, Arlene Pettifogger, ushered them into the outer office. "Are you the children who gave my nephew Jimmy money to buy new toys?"

"Yep," Isabella said. "That was us. And now we're here because we invented a new gum flavor for the flavor contest. We entered a while ago, but we never heard anything back."

Mr. Wigglesworth opened his office door. "Are these the ladies with the suggestion, Miss Pettifogger?"

"Oh, they are indeed. But, Mr. Wigglesworth, I want to tell you something. These girls ran a car wash and raised money to give my nephew. The Pettifoggers lost their roof, you know, in that twister. It was so kind of the kids to give that money to Jimmy and his parents. You girls should be very proud of what you did."

"Uh, thank you," said Deborah, nudging Isabella.

"Yeah. Thank you. But that's not why we came, Mr. Wigglesworth. I heard about your problem from my mom—I mean about how you need a new flavor of gum to keep the factory from closing down. Having the factory close would be really bad news for the town of Center Longnose, plus bad for my family, since we'd never be able to get that above-ground pool we have on layaway—"

"Psst. The gum!" Deborah whispered urgently.

"Oh. Right. So I had this idea for a new flavor of gum. It was before the tornado. I was looking up at the stars in the backyard with my pink armadillo on my stomach . . ."

By this time, Deborah had handed Mr. Wigglesworth and Miss Pettifogger each a piece of fresh gum.

"Your turn," she said to Isabella.

Isabella gave each adult a plastic spoon with a scoop of peanut butter. "Now, if y'all would please go ahead and chew that till the flavor is gone, it would help. You see, we weren't able to mix our new flavor with the gum at home. But you could do that here. Peanut-butter chewing gum. That's our idea."

"Yes. Hmmm. Interesting texture," said Mr. Wigglesworth, chewing thoughtfully as he combined the two.

"Yes, that slight crunch is unique. We Americans do like a crunch," added Miss Pettifogger.

"Easy enough to get peanuts to make this," he said. "Much easier than getting gallons of wintergreen oil."

"The flavor. Mmm. Not nearly as sweet as the mints and fruits."

"No. A little tang of salt instead. We could call it Grunch: the Gum with a Crunch. How about that? It comes with its own slogan!" Mr. Wigglesworth beamed. "No need to pay for advertising."

"And," said Deborah, "there could be vitamins in every piece. My mother would definitely buy gum with vitamins added in."

Mr. Wigglesworth called Amelia Wafflefoote, the lab director, into his office and gave her some gum and peanut butter.

"This is just terrific, girls," she said. She came forward to shake their hands. "Thank you very much."

"But, er, Mr. Wigglesworth?" Isabella said. "We sent this suggestion in for the contest. See, if we don't win this, then the pool—ow!"

Deborah had stepped on Isabella's toe, to keep her from rattling on and on about the pool.

Mr. Wigglesworth blushed. "Uh, yes. Well, I looked at your idea. But I didn't know it was as well

thought out as this . . . There wasn't a piece of gum for me to try included with your proposal, so I more or less overlooked it, I suppose."

"Well, we certainly owe them the contest award," said Amelia Wafflefoote. "Eh, Ernest?"

"You do have to be fair, sir," said Miss Pettifogger. "This is by far the best idea we got. Popular flavor? Supply not an issue? A slogan all ready to go? Grunch, the gum with a crunch?"

Would they give her the reward money? Isabella wondered. Her smile felt tight on her face. Her teeth were clenched tightly together.

"Quite right. If you'll excuse us, girls, we need to talk among ourselves for a moment. Would you kindly wait in the hall?"

Isabella sped madly up and down the hall while Deborah chewed her fingernails. "When I'm totally stressed," Deborah said, "I bite my nails."

"Oh. Yeah." Isabella was barely listening. "Can you imagine if we buy that pool? What a great summer we'll have!"

"You mean you're definitely inviting me to swim in it?" Deborah asked, sounding surprised.

"Well, yeah. Of course!" Isabella stared at her friend. "You mean you did all this work and helped me and came here, and all that time you thought you couldn't swim in the pool?"

"Well, I wasn't absolutely sure. I helped you just to . . . I don't know. Just to help you! I like helping people. It's fun."

"You think so? Yes. I guess it is."

Isabella stopped speedwalking. Inviting Deborah to swim in the pool all summer didn't feel the way being *forced* to share felt. Not at all. It felt perfectly natural. Perfectly wonderful!

"How could I possibly enjoy the pool without a friend like you to share the fun with?" Isabella threw her arms around Deborah and hugged her.

"I really don't know!" Deborah grinned.

The door to the lab opened. Miss Pettifogger ushered them back inside.

"Let's get right to it. Do you guys like the gum flavor or not?" Isabella asked, not able to wait a minute longer.

"We do indeed. Great concept. We'd like to award you the two-hundred-dollar bonus for the best gum-flavor idea."

Isabella screamed. She leaped into the air. She finally had the money for the pool!

"Hooray! Hooray!" both girls shouted, holding each other's hands and dancing in a circle.

13

When Isabella woke up the next day, she remembered that she still had one more problem. Deborah might be her best friend, and they finally had the pool money. But today, Wednesday, April 26, was kickball game day.

Isabella was pitcher.

And the boys in her class were not happy.

She dressed quickly in shorts, sneakers, and white jock socks. She put on a baseball cap to block out the sun glare. There.

She was too nervous to eat much breakfast.

One terrible thing about being a kid, Isabella thought as she and Deborah trudged to school that morning, was that no matter what important things were going on, you still had to go to school. She'd have to listen to Mrs. Wigglesworth nag about quiet and fuss about messiness. And she knew the boys were going to torture her about pitching.

Sure enough, right after attendance, Jed raised his hand. "Excuse me, Mrs. Wigglesworth. The kickball game is today. As we all know, Isabella never takes turns," Jed said. "She's the school's biggest swing hogger. And she does it on purpose. Her motto is . . . On the count of three, everybody: one, two, three!"

"I won't share 'cuz it's not fair," the boys shouted in unison.

"Hey! Wait, everyone!" Jimmy said loudly. "That's not true anymore. Isabella, Deborah, Nicky, and Marco donated a lot of money to me and my family. They earned it all by themselves."

"Yes. I heard about that," said the teacher. "Now, Jed, if you're trying to get me to change my mind about who pitches this afternoon, it just won't work. Isabella has as much right as anybody to pitch, especially after what she, Deborah, Nicky, and Marco did to help Jimmy. My decision is final." Mrs. Wigglesworth glared sternly at Jed.

Isabella looked down. She wouldn't give up being pitcher. She shouldn't give it up. She felt ready. She'd practiced as much as she could in order to do her part as well as she could. She'd do okay. Not great, maybe, but okay.

"Take out your spelling workbooks," said Mrs. Wigglesworth. "Turn to page 180, and remember, neatness counts, boys and girls."

Isabella sighed. She thought of the colossal mess

in her room. Maybe neatness did count. She dug her pencil from her desk and started on her word list.

The game was set for 1:35 that afternoon. At lunch recess, no one would play with her, because the boys still wanted her to give up her position. Glumly, she had told Deborah to hang out with someone else that day, since the boys were also pressuring Deborah to make Isabella back down.

Maybe Isabella could avoid the whole situation by pretending to be sick and getting sent home. She folded her arms across her stomach and walked around the playground doubled over, groaning.

She almost bumped into Jed. She looked up. He didn't seem very happy, either. He wasn't playing with anyone. He was kicking small stones into the storm drain and scowling. Then she had an idea, a trade-off idea.

"Hey, Jed! Listen."

"Yeah. What?" he asked ungraciously.

"It's about the game. Umm. I was wondering if maybe . . ."

"Yeah?"

"Well, maybe we could work something out. I know I used to say I hated sharing, but I don't really hate it. I mean, I did for a little while. But now it's okay. Especially if you get to decide how to do it yourself without other people forcing you. So I thought maybe I could pitch a few innings, and then—"

"You mean I could be relief pitcher? Wow. What a great idea! But, listen, let's keep it a secret so the fourth grade doesn't suspect our strategy. They'll all get used to you, and then suddenly they'll be facing me. I bet we wallop them. Thanks, Isabella!" He slapped her on the back.

Game time arrived. After all that practicing—with the Gatorade bottles, the tree trunk, and so on—Isabella's pitching really wasn't too bad. But her kicking was stupendous! No one else could kick the ball as high and as far as she could.

Everyone was amazed. The third graders began to chant "Speedwalker-Juarez, go, girl, go!" whenever she got her turn to kick. Even so, the game was tied all the way through the fourth inning, 7–7.

But the fourth grade was caught completely off guard when, in the fifth inning, Isabella stepped down from the mound and sat on the bench. They stared in disbelief as Jed took over.

"She's sharing," someone whispered. "Yeah. Wow. She was an okay pitcher. But she's sitting out and letting him have a turn. Jed'll shut them out. You watch. And she'll boot in a couple of runs. The fourth grade is doomed."

At the close of the class period the game ended, 15–7, third graders. Everyone was slapping Isabella high fives. They even tried to pick her up and carry her across the field over their heads. But it didn't work out.

"Thanks, guys. And when I get my above-ground pool set up, I'm going to have a splash party. You're all invited."

Afterward Isabella went straight over to Zach's. He was hammering the studs for the third wall of the new shop. The fourth wall would be a wide, garage-like door. Isabella sat on the pile of two-by-fours and heaved a deep sigh. "Well, I booted in two home runs at kickball today against the fourth grade. We won."

"Hey, that's terrific. Here, Isabella. Help me stand this wall up."

Together they pushed the third wall into place. Zach placed two temporary braces against it. Then Isabella held it steady while he began to toenail it into place. The six window holes, two on the third wall, were simply rectangular openings. Windows would come later.

"There. That's perfect. Thanks, Izzy-gator."

Finally, that very afternoon, Isabella, her mom, Zach, and Dozer drove in Zach's pickup truck down to Ray Baddeal's discount store and bought the long-awaited above-ground pool. Afterward her mom and Zach sat on the back deck sipping iced tea and talking.

Well, howdy, thought Isabella. Mom could use a good friend, besides me.

14

They didn't get the pool set up until the first week in May. First a circular spot in the backyard had to be leveled. Then every pebble had to be removed, and the lumps evened out. A layer of sand was spread next.

Then the pool had to be constructed. The blue vinyl liner had a powerful plastic smell. It took a few days to fill the pool with water. A few more to get the chlorine just right. And another day to let the water warm up to a comfortable temperature.

And finally, on Memorial Day weekend, with the water warm enough, most of Mrs. Wigglesworth's third grade came over for a great big backyard Texas barbecue with ribs and wings, tacos and nachos, and corn bread and six different kinds of barbecue sauce. For the occasion, Zach had very kindly lugged his picnic table next door again.

Their parents drove up to the curb in front of the Speedwalker-Juarez house and dropped off the children, who raced across the yard in bathing suits, T-shirts, and flip-flops, dropping their towels and flinging off their shirts as they ran.

The kids couldn't wait to get into the pool. They jumped and splashed and fell backward and had water fights and hollered until they were hoarse and the sun began to fade in the west.

"Thanks for inviting us, Isabella!" shouted Jimmy Pettifogger. "This is great."

"Hooray for Isabella!" yelled Nicky.

Everyone cheered three times and then went right back to leaping and hollering and splashing without a care in the world.

"That barbecue's almost ready. Food should settle them down. And after they eat, we'll send everybody home," Isabella's mom said to Granny and Zach.

"Yep. I can't wait for that. My dogs have had it," Granny answered.

"Phew, criminy. Let's not do that again anytime soon," Isabella's mother said when all the kids except Deborah had left. She and Isabella wearily tossed watermelon rinds and paper plates into the garbage can.

"I thought it was fun," Isabella said.

"It was great!" Deborah said.

"Phew, criminy!" Dozer said, throwing paper cups into the garbage can.

Isabella laughed.

"Well, I better go home now," Deborah said. "Thank you all for inviting me. Bye-bye."

"Bye, Deborah."

Now the yard was quiet. Dozer, Isabella, Zach, and Isabella's mom sat at the picnic table, just taking in the silence. Later, Granny made dinner and Zach joined them.

"Let's lie on our backs and watch the stars come out," said Isabella after dinner. "I like doing that."

Granny offered to clean up while Isabella, Dozer, their mom, and Zach lay in two rows on the picnic table, their feet resting on the benches, their heads at the center of the table.

"There's one!" said Isabella, pointing straight above them at a tiny blue star-flower.

"Okay, Isabella. First star. Make a wish," her mom said.

Isabella thought for a moment. Tomorrow they'd clean the pool and fix the chemicals. She had a best friend, Deborah, and she was getting along fine with her classmates. The Longnose Gum factory would stay in business. And there was a whiff of chlorine in the evening air and the hum of the circulator pump in her ears.

"You know what?" Isabella said. "Right now, I don't have a wish. I think everything's just about right."